SHOBO
GEORGE KAMBADAIS

BUCKHEAD™

Published by
BOOM! BOX™

Ross Richie ... Chairman & Founder
Jen Harned ... CFO
Matt Gagnon ... Editor-in-Chief
Filip Sablik ... President, Publishing & Marketing
Stephen Christy ... President, Development
Lance Kreiter ... Vice President, Licensing & Merchandising
Bryce Carlson ... Vice President, Editorial & Creative Strategy
Hunter Gorinson ... Vice President, Business Development
Josh Hayes ... Vice President, Sales
Sierra Hahn ... Executive Editor
Eric Harburn ... Executive Editor
Ryan Matsunaga ... Director, Marketing
Stephanie Lazarski ... Director, Operations
Elyse Strandberg ... Manager, Finance
Michelle Ankley ... Manager, Production Design
Cheryl Parker ... Manager, Human Resources
Dafna Pleban ... Senior Editor
Elizabeth Brei ... Editor
Kathleen Wisneski ... Editor
Sophie Philips-Roberts ... Editor
Allyson Gronowitz ... Associate Editor
Gavin Gronenthal ... Assistant Editor
Gwen Waller ... Assistant Editor
Ramiro Portnoy ... Assistant Editor
Kenzie Rzonca ... Assistant Editor
Rey Netschke ... Editorial Assistant
Marie Krupina ... Design Lead
Crystal White ... Design Lead
Grace Park ... Design Coordinator
Madison Goyette ... Production Designer
Veronica Gutierrez ... Production Designer
Jessy Gould ... Production Designer
Nancy Mojica ... Production Designer
Samantha Knapp ... Production Design Assistant
Esther Kim ... Marketing Lead
Breanna Sarpy ... Marketing Lead, Digital
Amanda Lawson ... Marketing Coordinator
Alex Lorenzen ... Marketing Coordinator, Copywriter
Grecia Martinez ... Marketing Assistant, Digital
José Meza ... Consumer Sales Lead
Ashley Troub ... Consumer Sales Coordinator
Harley Salbacka ... Sales Coordinator
Megan Christopher ... Operations Lead
Rodrigo Hernandez ... Operations Coordinator
Jason Lee ... Senior Accountant
Faizah Bashir ... Business Analyst
Amber Peters ... Staff Accountant
Sabrina Lesin ... Accounting Assistant

BOOM! BOX™

BUCKHEAD Volume One, September 2022. Published by BOOM! Box, a division of Boom Entertainment, Inc. Buckhead is ™ & © 2022 Shobo Coker & George Kambadais. Originally published in single magazine form as BUCKHEAD No. 1-5. ™ & © 2021 Shobo Coker & George Kambadais. All rights reserved. BOOM! Box™ and the BOOM! Box logo are trademarks of Boom Entertainment, Inc., registered in various countries and categories. All characters, events, and institutions depicted herein are fictional. Any similarity between any of the names, characters, persons, events, and/or institutions in this publication to actual names, characters, and persons, whether living or dead, events, and/or institutions is unintended and purely coincidental. BOOM! Box does not read or accept unsolicited submissions of ideas, stories, or artwork.

BOOM! Studios, 5670 Wilshire Boulevard, Suite 400, Los Angeles, CA 90036-5679. Printed in China. First Printing.

ISBN: 978-1-68415-847-8, eISBN: 978-1-64668-594-3

WRITTEN BY SHOBO
ART BY GEORGE KAMBADAIS
LETTERED BY JIM CAMPBELL

COVER BY
GEORGE KAMBADAIS

COLLECTION DESIGNER
VERONICA GUTIERREZ

SERIES DESIGNER
GRACE PARK

ASSISTANT EDITOR
KENZIE RZONCA

EDITOR
SOPHIE PHILIPS-ROBERTS

SENIOR EDITOR
SHANNON WATTERS

LEVEL ONE

CREATE YOUR CHARACTER

NAME: TOBA

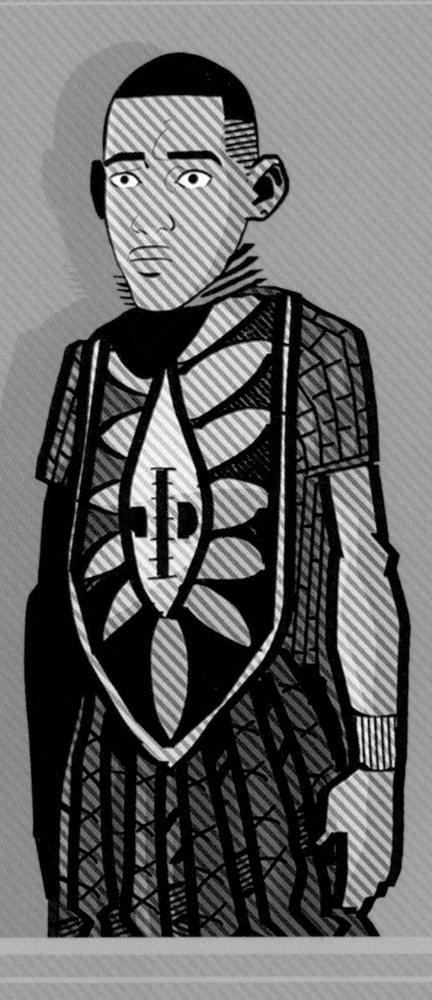

FACE

BODY

HAIR

STRENGTH

VITALITY

CHARISMA

INTELLECT

AGILITY

LUCK

A DIG SITE, DEEP BENEATH THE JUNGLE ON THE OUTSKIRTS OF BENIN CITY, NIGERIA.
"HAS NO ONE EVER EXCAVATED THIS DEEP?"
"NEVER, BOLA. WE'RE IN THE **HEART OF THE OLD EDO KINGDOM** NOW!"
ARE YOU GETTING THESE SCANS, WOLE?
YUP!
MEREDITH, REPOSITION THE OTHER LIDAR SCANNER, WILL YOU?
THAT'S WEIRD.
IS THAT... ***LIGHT?***
GRRRRUUUUUNK
WHA--!
A SECRET MECHANISM!

RRRUMRUUMBLE
THE WALLS... ***THEY'RE PARTING!***

THAT THING... HOW IS IT *GLOWING,* BOLA?
I...I SEE IT, WOLE.
WELL! THIS WHOLE EXPEDITION JUST *PAID FOR ITSELF!*
WAIT 'TIL DAD HEARS ABOUT THIS!
NO, MEREDITH. WE AGREED YOU'D KEEP SAMUEL OUT OF THIS. I DON'T *TRUST* HIM.
YOU SURE? HE'D BE WILLING TO FUND THE ARCHIVAL PROJECT FOR YEA--
NOTHING'S LEAVING NIGERIA, MEREDITH.
WE DO THIS ON OUR OWN.

FINE. JUST MAKE SURE WOLE GETS THE SCANS WE NEED, AND YOU--
I'LL GET THE DATA WE NEED TO PROGRAM THE AI CHARACTERS. YES.
FINDING THIS THING--WHATEVER IT IS--DOESN'T *CHANGE* ANYTHING.

BOLA... WHATEVER IT IS, IT'S STILL ACTIVE!
OKAY. OKAY. BUT WHAT A THING!
WHAT DO YOU MEAN, ACTIVE?
I MEAN I'M DETECTING ELECTRICAL ACTIVITY.
GONNA GET A READING, SEE IF I CAN--
WOLE!
SHZZZLOP
WOLE!

BUCKHEAD, WASHINGTON.
ONE YEAR LATER.
TOBA!
TOBA ADEKUNLE!
I'M MODDING!
YOUR FRIEND'S HERE TO TAKE YOU TO SCHOOL!
FRIEND? I BARELY EVEN KNOW THE GUY!

UGH, NONE OF THESE SHIRTS ARE RIGHT...
...C'MON NOW, MAKE A DECISION.
WAIT, WHAT?

NO! NO! NO! NOT TODAY!
OF ALL DAYS!
IT'S YOUR FIRST DAY. DON'T BE LATE!
I'LL BE THERE IN A MINUTE!

HI, I'M TOBA.
NOPE, NOT TOW-BA.
TOH-BA. RHYMES WITH... TOH-BA.
FORGET IT.
NOW... TO POP, OR NOT TO POP?

MORNING, MUM. UH... JOSUE, RIGHT?
YEAH! HI!
EAT QUICKLY, TOBA. JOSUE CAME ALL THE WAY HERE TO--
NO. AH-AH. NO WAY!
YOU ARE NOT WEARING THAT SHIRT TO SCHOOL!
INTERESTED
WHAT'S GOTTEN INTO YOU? I NEED YOU TO BE SUPPORTIVE RIGHT NOW.
WE COULD HAVE MOVED ANYWHERE.
STONE INDUSTRIES HAS OFFICES IN NEW YORK AND CHICAGO, BUT YOU HAD TO CHOOSE THE MIDDLE OF NOWHERE?
CHANGE YOUR SHIRT. NOW.

MOMS, RIGHT? SHEESH!
MY MOM'S ALWAYS ON MY CASE, TOO. "DO THIS! DO THAT! HOW ARE YOU EVER GONNA BE AN ACCOUNTANT IF YOU DON'T--"

WHOOOOA!
WHO LIVES IN *THAT* HOUSE?!

LIVES IN WHAT HOUSE? THE EMPTY LOT?
EMPTY LOT? **THAT HOUSE RIGHT THERE!**
I DON'T SEE WHAT-- *WOAH!*
HEY, WHERE ARE YOU GOING?
WE'LL BE LATE FOR SCHOOL. IT'S JUST AN EMPT--
STOP WORRYING, WE WON'T BE...
...LATE.

WHAT ARE YOU DOING?
DUDE, C'MON, WHY AREN'T YOU MOVING?
THIS ISN'T FUNNY.

WOW! NOT EVEN BLINKING...
I'M GOING TO POKE YOUR EYE!
MY FINGER'S GETTING REEEAL CLOSE. CLOSER!
SQUISH!
EUGH! SORRY, SORRY! DIDN'T REALLY MEAN... WOW! THAT'S COMMITMENT!
YOUR MUM LET YOU GET A TATTOO? STRANGE DESI--
HEY! YOU!

YOU'RE ON MY PROPERTY! EXPLAIN HOW.
I WASN'T SURE ANYONE LIVED HERE. SAW YOUR HOUSE FROM ACROSS THE STREET AND--
DON'T COME ANY CLOSER. THAT'S FAR ENOUGH!
WAIT... I DON'T KNOW YOU. YOU'RE... NEW!
UH, YEAH, I JUST MOVED HERE FROM--
SHOW ME YOUR NECK.
WHAT ARE YOU, A VAMPIRE?
THE TATTOO, DUMBASS! SHOW IT TO ME.

I DON'T... HAVE A TATTOO? MY FRIEND DOES...
GET 'EM, SHADOW!
BORK! BORK!
BORK!
BORK!
BRRF! WHAT ARE YOU--
OOOGHF!
BORK!
WHAT HAPPENED BACK THERE?
TELL YOU LATER! GOTTA GO! GOTTA GO! SCHOOL, REMEMBER?

TOWBA?
TOBA.
TO--TTT...
TOR-BA?
TOH-BA.
...OKAY!
EVERYONE GIVE A WARM BUCKHEAD MIDDLE SCHOOL WELCOME TO...TOWBA!
HI, TOWBA.
HI, TOBA!
WE'RE NEW, TOO. SAME THING HAPPENED TO ME. NAME'S ROMY, STAR WRESTLER.
MEL. DON'T SWEAT IT, TOBA.
YOU PRONOUNCED MY NAME RIGHT!
IF I CAN PRONOUNCE MR. BEVILACQUA, I CAN PRONOUNCE TOBA.

"COME ON, TOBA. LET ME TAKE YOU ON THE CERTIFIED JOSUE TOUR OF BUCKHEAD MIDDLE SCHOOL!"
"OUR FIRST STOP: GYM. THE SWEAT-SOAKED ARMPIT OF HADES.
"ALGEBRA. WHERE TINY BITS OF YOUR SOUL WILL BE BLASTED AWAY..."
"...ONE EQUATION AT A TIME."
"BUT I LOVE ALGEBRA!"
"FINE, TOBA, ALGEBRA'S NOT BAD IF YOU'RE A WEIRDO. BUT THERE'S STILL U.S. GOVERNMENT...
"LITERATURE...
"ECONOMICS..."
RIIIIIIIING

THE LUNCHROOM! REFUGE OF THE POOR, OVERWORKED MASSES.
YOUR MOM FIXED YOU LUNCH?!
WISH MY MOM MADE ME LUNCH.
SHARE?

WHAT'S UP NEXT?
SOCIAL STUDIES. BORING, BUG-EYED BEVILACQUA.
MEL!

WHAT? I'VE SEEN HIM. DUDE HAS LIKE... MASSIVE EYE SOCKETS!
WANNA SKIP CLASS? CHECK OUT THE COMPUTER LAB?
OH! THAT'S NOT A GOOD IDEA.
THEY'RE UPGRADING THE LAB. WE'RE NOT ALLOWED IN THERE.
WE'LL GET IN SO MUCH TROUBLE!

HEY, WE CAN'T BE IN HERE.
YEAH, WE CAN. LOOK, I'M IN HERE.
YOOO! WHY DOES OUR COMPUTER LAB SMELL LIKE ROTTEN EGGS?
CHAI! THESE COMPUTERS ARE STATE-OF-THE-ART!
AAAAND THERE'S NOT A SINGLE GAME INSTALLED.
"EDUTAINMENT" SOFTWARE.
SO WE SHOULD HEAD BACK NOW, RIGHT?
UH... WHAT'S THAT?
WHAT'S IN THERE?
I MEAN... WE HAVE TO TAKE A LOOK, RIGHT?

IT'S PROBABLY JUST JANITOR STUFF, RIGHT?
WE SHOULD PROBABLY GET TO CLASS.
KA-THUNK-GRRRRRR
CHECK. IT. OUT!
BRO! THAT AIN'T JANITOR STUFF.
JOSUE. YOU HAVE THE COOLEST SCHOOL. EVER.
I DON'T... WHAT IS THIS PLACE?

tik-Pak-a! Pik-tak-tak!
THIS OPERATING SYSTEM IS... STRANGE.
IT'S LIKE... IT KNOWS WHAT I WANT TO DO BEFORE I DO IT.
Elseverse.exe
"ELSEVERSE"?
CLICK ON IT.
IT'S A GAME. IS IT AFRICAN?
YEAH. IT'S SET IN BENIN. THE OLD EDO KINGDOM!
MY...DAD USED TO STUDY THE PLACE WITH MY MUM, BEFORE HE DISAPPEARED.
HE'D... LOVE THIS.
MY DAD'S GONE TOO.
NOT GONE. JUST... MISSING.
WANT TO PLAY?

CREATE YOUR CHARACTER
NAME: |
FACE
BODY
HAIR
STRENGTH
VITALITY
CHARISMA
INTELLECT
AGILITY
LUCK
"CAN'T GET MY HAIR RIGHT. THEY NEVER GET THE HAIR RIGHT..."
"YOU CHOSE A HEALER, TOBA? PSHH!"
"THESE GRAPHICS ARE INCREDIBLE!"
"IS IT AFRICAN?"

"...TOLD YOU NOT TO KITE THEM, ROMY!"
"MEL, JUMP! JUMP! NO, WAIT, DON'T JUMP!"
"WOULD YOU LET ME THINK, PEOPLE!"
"THAT DOG-THING'S GONNA GET YOU!"
TOBA! IS THAT YOU?
D...DAD?!
RIIIIING

WHAT...?
AW, MAN!
WELP, THAT'S THE BELL. GOTTA GO! RIGHT?
FINE. FINE. THIS GAME'S FUN THOUGH! ROMY LIKE!
DON'T EVER REFER TO YOURSELF IN THE THIRD PERSON. EVER.
WE SNEAK IN AFTER-HOURS, AND PLAY SOME MORE.

SURE, NOT LIKE I NEED SLEEP.
YOU OKAY, BUDDY? YOU SEEM... SPOOKED.
HE'S FINE.
I'M FINE, JUST... I THOUGHT I SAW SOMETHING IN THERE. SAW SOMEONE.
JOSUE, YOU'RE IN, RIGHT?
I DUNNO--

SETTLED THEN! MEET UP IN FRONT OF JOSUE'S AT 10!

KERRRRRAKOW
REALLY? NO ONE SHOWS UP! C'MON, JOSUE!
22:15

HUH? JOSUE'S PARENTS!
THEY'RE JUST...STARING AT EACH OTHER...
THAT'S... UNSETTLING...

TATTOO?!

BETTER CHECK ON JOSUE.
CRAZY-HOBO-GIRLS, WEIRD COMPUTER GAMES...
WHAT A TOWN...

MUM?!
MMMPFFH!

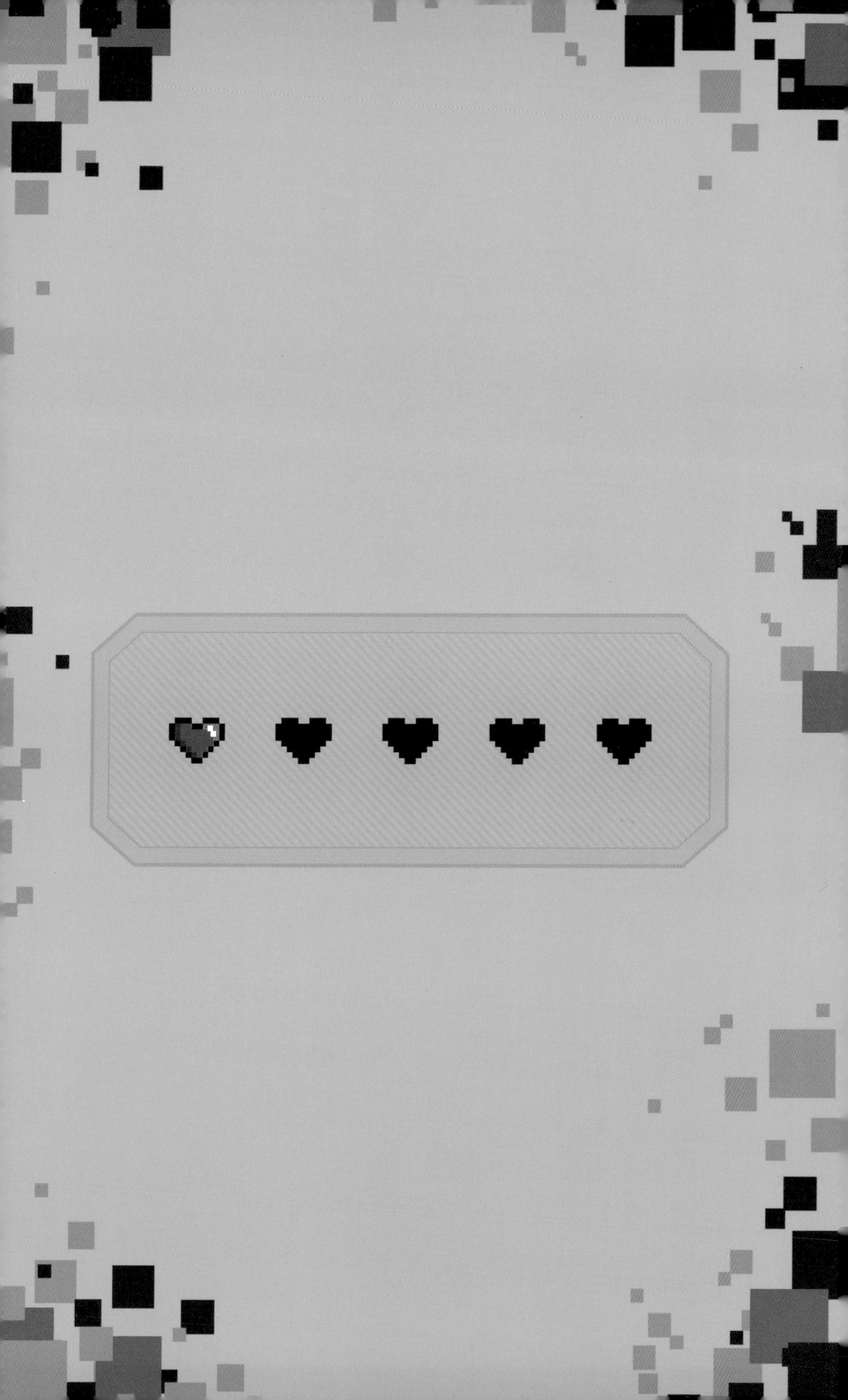

LEVEL TWO

CREATE YOUR CHARACTER

NAME: JOSUE

FACE

BODY

HAIR

STRENGTH

VITALITY

CHARISMA

INTELLECT

AGILITY

LUCK

KRRRACKOW
WAH-AAAGH!
UNFFF!
SPLARCH
THAT WASN'T MUM...
WHO WAS THAT?
WHAT WERE THEY DOING TO JOSUE?!

WHAM
MUM! MUM?!
SHE ISN'T HERE... SHE ISN'T HERE?! THEY TOOK MUM!
CALM DOWN, TOBA. CALL THE POLICE.
beep beeeep
NO SIGNAL?!
NO! NO! NO!

KERRRAKOW

CRASH

THE ADEKUNLE HOME IN LAGOS, NOT LONG AGO.
WE'RE GOING TO AMERICA? COOL!
THE COMPANY YOUR DAD AND I USED TO WORK FOR OFFERED ME A POSITION.
YOU REMEMBER AUNTIE MEREDITH? SHE HAS SOME...DATA SHE'D LIKE ME TO TAKE A LOOK AT.
THAT'S SO COOL! NEW YORK? CHICAGO?
WASHINGTON. BUT WE HAVE TO LEAVE TOMORROW.
WOW, WASHINGTON DC...!
IT'S GOOD TO SEE YOU HAPPY AGAIN, TOBA.

TOBA! YOU'RE SO CLOSE!
I NEED YOUR HELP!
TOBA! **HELP MEEEEE!**
BANG
BANG

BANG
BANG
BANG
THERE HE IS! BEEN HERE TEN MIN--
WOAH... WHAT HAPPENED TO YOU?!
WHAT HAPPENED TO ME?
YOU NEVER SHOWED UP LAST NIGHT!
NO, YOU NEVER SHOWED UP!
I DID! MEL AND ROMY DIDN'T SHOW EITHER, SO I CLIMBED UP TO YOUR BEDROOM WINDOW--
YOU CLIMBED UP TO MY BEDROOM WINDOW?

SHHHH! DON'T SHOUT, THEY'LL HEAR US!
WHO WILL HEAR US?
THE GOONS IN THE BLACK SUITS!
THERE'S SOMETHING GOING ON IN THIS TOWN, JOSUE. SOMETHING BAD.
I THINK THEY TOOK MY MUM OR...
OR SHE'S INVOLVED, SOMEHOW. I DON'T...
OKAY. I BELIEVE YOU.
BUT DUDE, YOU GOTTA GET CHANGED.
I'LL FIX YOU LUNCH, WE'LL TALK ABOUT IT ON THE WAY TO SCHOOL.

...AND THEN THEY GRABBED MUM, AND I RAN HOME...
...AND WHEN I LOOKED OUT THE WINDOW, I SAW THEM. WATCHING!
WHEN YOU SAW YOUR MOM, WAS SHE...HURTING ME?
I DON'T KNOW. I DON'T THINK SO. YOU WERE ASLEEP.
I FEEL FINE.
YOUR MOM'S CAR WAS GONE WHEN I GOT TO YOUR PLACE THIS MORNING. MUST HAVE GONE TO WORK ALREADY.
MAYBE THEY TOOK IT WITH THEM WHEN THEY LEFT.
MUM'S CELL PHONE'S DEAD, TOO.
I THINK THEY HAVE HER, JOSUE.
I SAW THEM. I'M NOT IMAGINING THINGS.
I KNOW.
THAT'S WHAT'S FREAKING ME OUT.

HEY, WHERE ARE MEL AND ROMY?
DUNNO. Y-YOU THINK THEY GOT 'EM TOO?
WC
YOU!
WHAT THE...?
STOP!
I NEED TO TALK TO YOU!

OOF!
OH DEAR!
SMASH
I'M VERY SORRY, SIR!
QUITE ALRIGHT, DON'T YOU WORRY, YOUNG MAN!
I'LL HELP YOU UP, MR...
MR... BEVILACQUA?
ARE YOU IN ONE OF MY CLASSES? I'M AFRAID I DON'T RECOGNIZE YOU...
NO. I'VE JUST... HEARD GOOD THINGS!
I'M TOBA.
I HOPE TO RUN INTO YOU AGAIN SOON, TOBA!
AHAHA! AHAHA! EH!?

SHE GOT AWAY. VANISHED.
SAME GIRL YOU SAID YOU SAW YESTERDAY?
SAME. SHE WAS FIDDLING WITH AN ELECTRICAL PANEL.
SO?
SO...YOU, YOUR MUM, YOUR DAD AND MR. BEVILACQUA ALL HAVE THOSE STRANGE ELECTRIC TATTOOS!
SHE ASKED ME IF I HAD ONE. DON'T YOU THINK THAT'S FISHY?
BEVILACQUA'S GOT A TATTOO? THAT IS WEIRD!
AHAHA!
OW! HAHA! YEAH, THAT'S WEIRD.
SERIOUSLY THOUGH, IT'S JUST A BIRTH-MARK.
JOSUE... THAT'S NO BIRTHMARK!

ANYWAY. I HAD A... WEIRD DREAM. I SAW MY DAD IN THE ELSEVERSE.
I THINK WE NEED TO PLAY THE ELSEVERSE GAME AGAIN.
ALRIGHT. LET'S GO. BEFORE I CHANGE MY MIND.
NEED TO GET MY FLASH DRIVE...
...SEE IF I CAN MAKE A COPY OF THE PROGRAM.
I WILL COME FOR YOU TONIGHT
WHAT'S THIS?
THIS IS GETTING OUTTA HAND...
COME ON. LET'S GET TO THE COMPUTER LAB.

TH-THE STORAGE ROOM...IT'S GONE!
THAT'S IMPOSSIBLE!
LOOK! IT'S WET. FRESH PAINT!
HERE'S WHAT WE'RE GONNA DO.
WE MEET UP AT YOUR PLACE FTER SCHOOL, AND WE GET HESE BLACK SUITS ON VIDEO.
GET EVIDENCE, GO TO THE COPS. OKAY?
OKAY. THANKS, JOSUE.

FOOTPRINTS. THE GOONS ARE REAL. I KNEW IT!
COME ON, JOSUE. WHERE ARE YOU?
19:07

BETTER CHECK MUM'S ROOM. SEE IF I CAN FIND ANYTHING...
WHAT'S THIS?
snik snak
The Else Virtual Reality System
A better way to remember
"ELSE VIRTUAL REALITY SYSTEM."
WHAT WERE MUM AND DAD WORKING ON?

Wole and I designed the Elseverse to preserve our country's history. We wanted to recreate every detail as accurately as possible.
So, we traveled the country, scanning ruins and relics. Wole rebuilt the ancient worlds virtually, and I developed the AI to populate them.
It was bliss...
...'til we ran out of money.
Enter Stone Industries. Meredith Stone and her father, ***Samuel.***
Samuel said he wanted to use the data to build a VR tourism app.
But then we discovered an... ***intelligence,*** deep in the ruins of the Edo Kingdom.
It took Wole's mind, and left his body broken.

Samuel said he could help. I let him take Wole's body to America.
I stayed in Nigeria with Toba, while Meredith studied Wole.
Then, one day, she sent me a message—***The intelligence is talking.*** It has taken Wole ***hostage.***
I AM EWON.
I designed the BSP-Pak as ***a bridge into the Elseverse.*** I will meet up with Meredith, we'll find this Ewon, and I will ***make*** him release my husband.
BANG BANG
TOBA! TOBA! I'M HOME!

PHEW! IT'S WINDY, SHA!
SORRY I'M LATE.
IS...THAT A CHAIR LEG?
M... MUM?
HAVE YOU BEEN GETTING INTO TROUBLE?
I THOUGHT YOU WERE GONE. I THOUGHT THEY HAD YOU!
WHERE WERE YOU?

SORRY I DIDN'T MAKE IT HOME LAST NIGHT, WE HAD A BREAKTHROUGH AT THE LAB.
DIDN'T YOU GET MY TEXT?
TEXT? NO, I...I THOUGHT THEY HAD YOU. THOUGHT HE HAD YOU...
HE? WHO'S HE?
...EWON?!
...
YES, EWON. AND BUTTERMAN. AND BEVILACQUA.
AND JOSUE.

YOUR MOTHER WAS STRONG. DIFFICULT TO CONTROL.
BUT SHE SUCCUMBED, AS WILL YOU.
WHAT ARE YOU?
I AM THE CHAIN THAT BINDS. YOUR ANCESTORS KNEW ME WELL.
YOU WILL KNOW ME AGAIN.
YOU WISH TO SEE YOUR FATHER? THEN COME. IT IS EASIER IF YOU DO NOT STRUGGLE...
SER-KRACK

GASP
I GOTTA GET OUTTA HERE!
click
BRAAAKSH

AAARGH!
AAHHH!
BORK! BORK!
I TOLD YOU I'D COME FOR YOU TONIGHT.
C'MON, KID. WE HAVE WORK TO DO!

LEVEL THREE

CREATE YOUR CHARACTER

NAME: DARSHA

FACE

BODY

HAIR

STRENGTH

VITALITY

CHARISMA

INTELLECT

AGILITY

LUCK

BORK!
BORK!
GROOOAAAN!
YEAH, HE'S ALRIGHT.
GET UP, KID.

HEY, SLEEPING BEAUTY!
DARSHA SAYS YOU RAN INTO BEVILACQUA?
YEAH, AND HE GOT MY NAME RIGHT!
IT'S SO GOOD TO SEE YOU TWO!
TOBA, YOU HAD US WORRIED, BRO!

IS THAT...
JOSUE?!

HAD TO TIE HIM UP. YOUR FRIEND'S NOT HIMSELF.
MEL AND ROMY RESCUED HIM WHILE I CAME FOR YOU.
DON'T WORRY, WE'VE BEEN LOOKING AFTER HIM.
THERE ARE ENOUGH OF US NOW. WE'RE GONNA FIGHT BACK!
SHE'S LIKE...UBER-DOOMSDAY-PREPPER-PERSON.
WHO PUT YOU IN CHARGE?
OH, SHE'S DEFINITELY IN CHARGE.
I'M ALSO THE ONLY ONE WHO KNOWS WHAT THE HELL IS GOING ON IN BUCKHEAD!
SNIFF
SNIFF
YOU GET USED TO THE SMELL.
SPEAK FOR YOURSELF.

"I WAS IN GYM CLASS WHEN IT STARTED. WHEN THE **ROBOTS IN BLACK SUITS** FIRST ATTACKED--"
"**ANDROIDS.** THEY'RE HUMANOID. ALL ANDROIDS ARE ROBOTS, NOT ALL ROBOTS ARE ANDROIDS."
"WHEN THE **ROBOTS** ATTACKED, I HID...
"...AND I FOUGHT.
"THE ROBOTS GOT EVERYONE ELSE.
"EVERYONE, EVEN MY PARENTS.
"SO I RAN.
"I SAVED SHADOW.
"WELL, **HE SAVED ME.**"
BORK!
BORK!

"I HID HERE, IN THIS OLD, ABANDONED HOUSE... THE BUNKER.
"I SET UP BOOBY TRAPS, JUST IN CASE."
"BOOBY TRAPS?!"
"RELAX, I HAD SHADOW CHASE YOU OFF BEFORE YOU COULD HURT YOURSELF, DIDN'T I?
"ANYWAY, I STARTED SNEAKING INTO HOUSES AT NIGHT TO SCAVENGE FOR FOOD.
"THAT'S WHEN I FOUND OUT THE GROWN-UPS ARE MIND-CONTROLLED. AND THEY GO SOMEWHERE AT MIDNIGHT, EVERY NIGHT!
"SO I FOLLOWED THEM.
"FOUND OUT THEY GO TO THE SCHOOL.
"THEY'RE BUILDING SOMETHING, BUT I DON'T KNOW WHAT, AND I DON'T KNOW WHY."

"WHAT I DO KNOW IS THEY'RE BEING CONTROLLED FROM INSIDE THE SCHOOL.
"BY SOME KIND OF ELECTRONIC SIGNAL."
"THE TATTOOS! THAT'S HOW THEY'RE CONTROLLING EVERYONE."
MOM STARTED ACTING WEIRD A DAY OR TWO AFTER WE ARRIVED.
UH...YEAH, MY FOLKS TOO.
THEY'VE ALWAYS BEEN WEIRD, THOUGH.
"SO YOU THINK IT'S AN ELECTRONIC SIGNAL? IS THAT WHY YOU WERE FIDDLING WITH THE ELECTRICAL PANEL AT THE SCHOOL YESTERDAY?"
"I WAS TRYING TO TRACE THE SIGNAL TO THE CONTROL ROOM."
I BUILT THAT SIGNAL DAMPENER TO CLOAK THE BUNKER. IT INTERFERES WITH THE MIND-CONTROL SIGNAL.
THAT'S WHY JOSUE FROZE WHEN WE CAME BY THE OTHER DAY! WHY HE CAN'T EVEN SEE THIS PLACE!
THE DAMPENER'S THE ONLY THING STOPPING THE SIGNAL FROM REACHING THE OUTSIDE WORLD. KEEPS IT CONTAINED.
SO IF IT... BREAKS?
THE SIGNAL GETS OUT.

PLAN'S SIMPLE. GET TO THE SCHOOL, FIND THE CONTROL ROOM, AND DESTROY IT.
THE COMPUTER GAME IN THE SUB-BASEMENT!
THAT'S GOTTA BE THE CONTROL ROOM!
WHAT ARE WE WAITING FOR? LET'S GO!
NO! WAIT! YOU DON'T HAVE THE WHOLE PICTURE.
BELIEVE ME.
I FOUND THESE FILES IN MY MOM'S ROOM. THEY EXPLAIN WHO'S CONTROLLING EVERYONE IN BUCKHEAD.
I'LL TELL YOU EVERYTHING.

"ACCORDING TO YORUBA HISTORY, HIS NAME IS EWON, AND HE WAS ONE OF EIGHT GENERALS IN AN ANCIENT CELESTIAL ARMY CALLED THE AJOGUN.
"THE YORUBA PEOPLE SAY THAT IN THE ANCIENT KINGDOM OF THE EDO, THE AJOGUN FOUGHT AGAINST HUMANS AND OUR DIVINE PROTECTORS, THE ÒRÌSHÀ.
"THE AJOGUN WERE JEALOUS OF OUR FREEDOM. THEY WANTED TO FEED ON US, AND CORRUPT THE WORLD THE ÒRÌSHÀ CREATED."

"WHEN THE WAR WAS OVER AND THE AJOGUN WERE DEFEATED, THE ÒRÌSHÀ LEFT THE MORTAL WORLD.
"WELL, THEY THOUGHT THE WAR WAS OVER.
"THE AJOGUN WERE ONLY SLEEPING.
"WHEN THEY RETURNED, THEY FOUND HUMANS HAD BUILT MIGHTY CITIES.
"AND THEY LEARNED THE ÒRÌSHÀ HAD LEFT US UNPROTECTED.
"THEIR SPIES TOLD THE AJOGUN THAT HUMANS WERE EASILY DIVIDED. THAT WE DIDN'T KNOW HOW TO CARE FOR EACH OTHER."

"WITH THE ÒRÌSHÀ GONE, IT WAS THE PERFECT TIME FOR THE AJOGUN TO STRIKE.
"THEY SENT GENERAL EWON, THE SPIRIT OF IMPRISONMENT, TO THE LARGEST CITY IN THE LAND.
"WE BUILT STRONG WALLS TO KEEP HIM OUT. HE DESTROYED THEM.
"WE TRAINED THE BRAVEST WARRIORS. HE DEFEATED THEM."
HHSSSSSSS
"FEAR GRIPPED THE PEOPLE. WE SPLINTERED EVEN MORE, AND THAT MADE IT EASIER FOR EWON TO PICK US OFF.
"...AND OUR LEADERS, THE PEOPLE WE LOOKED TO FOR GUIDANCE? THEY ABANDONED US."

"THE OBA, THE KING, MADE A DARK BARGAIN.
"HE AGREED TO SACRIFICE A HUNDRED OF HIS PEOPLE TO KEEP EWON HAPPY.
"IT WAS NEVER ENOUGH FOR EWON. HE NEEDED TO FEED HIS CHILDREN--AN ARMY OF EVIL MINIONS FROM THE SHADOW REALM.
"THEN, ONE DAY, A WANDERING MATHEMATICIAN CAME TO THE COURT, AND PROMISED HE COULD IMPRISON EWON FOREVER.
"HE SUCCEEDED, TRAPPING EWON IN A FRACTAL MATH PUZZLE OF HIS OWN DESIGN.
"WELL, UNTIL MY MUM AND DAD FOUND THE SPHERE, FIVE HUNDRED YEARS LATER."

SO...YOUR DAD'S TRAPPED IN THE ELSEVERSE WITH THIS EVIL MONSTER... THING.
IN A MATH PUZZLE BOX.
IN THE BASEMENT OF OUR SCHOOL.
YEAH.
ALSO THESE NOTES SAY EWON'S ONE OF THE EIGHT WARLORDS OF CHAOS.
WELL, THIS JUST KEEPS GETTING BETTER AND BETTER.
DOESN'T MATTER. WE STOP HIM.
WE GET OUR FOLKS BACK.
YEAH, BUT HOW?
DID YA MISS THE EIGHT WARLORDS OF CHAOS PART?

THIS IS HOW. IT'S CALLED A BSP-PAK.
MUM DESIGNED IT. SHE WAS GOING TO USE IT TO ENTER THE ELSEVERSE AND RESCUE MY DAD.
NEVER GOT TO BUILD IT THOUGH.
LET ME HAVE A LOOK.
THIS IS A PRETTY ELEGANT DESIGN.
I THINK I CAN BUILD THIS THING.
C'MON, MAKE A CLEARING.
I'LL GET MY WELDING EQUIPMENT.
DID SHE SAY WELDING EQUIPMENT?
LET'S GET TO IT.

ZWWIP
POK
POK
SNIP
BORK!
WELL, IT'S NOT PRETTY.
BUT WE'LL SEE IF IT WORKS.
FRIZZ
FRRRZ

klik
WHOOM
WHOOOM
WHOOOOOM
IS IT SUPPOSED TO SOUND LIKE IT'S GONNA BLOW US UP?!
BORK! BORK!

I MADE A FEW MODIFICATIONS.
AS LONG YOU'RE IN CONTACT WITH THE PERSON WEARING IT, THE PAK'LL CLOAK YOU FROM THE BLACK SUITS...AND THE GROWN-UPS.
BUT... WE'VE ONLY GOT ONE PAK!
SO YOU'LL HAVE TO STAY CLOSE.
HEY, SO...YOU CAN'T SAVE THE WORLD ON AN EMPTY TUMMY.
GRMBL
-SIGH- I'VE BEEN GROWING VEGETABLES AND FRUIT IN THE BACKYARD.
I GUESS WE COULD FIX DINNER.
SEE? DOOMSDAY-PREPPER-PERSON!
YOU FOLKS GO AHEAD.
I'LL GET THE TABLE READY.

IT ISN'T EASY MAKING NEW FRIENDS.
THANKS FOR BEING COOL, JOSUE.
AND FOR SHOWING ME AROUND SCHOOL, EVEN WHEN YOU WERE SCARED.
I'M SORRY I GOT YOU INTO TROUBLE.
I MEAN... I FEEL LIKE THIS IS SORT OF MY FAULT.
OR MY MUM'S...? MAYBE DAD'S?
...I DON'T KNOW.
WISH THEY WERE HERE TO HELP ME.
HEY, TOBA. YOU'VE GOT US. WE'LL GET THEM ALL OUT.
LET'S GO SET THE TABLE.
OH, AND YOU KNOW I'M TELLING ROMY I SAW YOU CRY!

hahahahaha
ALRIGHT, TIME TO SUIT UP.
DUCT TAPE, SUPER GLUE, FLASHLIGHTS, WHATEVER YOU NEED, GRAB IT NOW.

REMEMBER, WE ONLY HAVE ONE PAK.
ONCE WE'RE OUTSIDE, THERE'LL BE GOONS AND GROWN-UPS EVERYWHERE.
WE CAN'T LET THEM SEE US...

"...SO HOLD ON TO EACH OTHER.
"DO NOT LET GO."
GROWN-UPS CAN'T SEE US. SO WEIRD.
SOMETIMES IT FEELS LIKE I'M ALWAYS INVISIBLE TO MY MOM.
WE'RE NOT INVISIBLE. THEY JUST CAN'T SEE US.
HEY, DARSHA! WHEN WE GET TO THE SCHOOL, GIVE ME THE PAK, OKAY?
I SHOULD BE THE ONE TO GO INTO THE ELSEVERSE.
NO.
WHAT? YOU DON'T EVEN KNOW WHAT MY DAD LOOKS LIKE.
I NEED TO GET HIM OUTTA THERE.
SHOW ME A PICTURE THEN.
I'VE BEEN HERE MONTHS BY MYSELF. I'M FINISHING THIS.

YEAH? MAYBE YOU SHOULD FIND YOUR OWN WAY TO THE CONTROL ROOM!
WHAT ARE YOU DOING? I TOLD YOU NOT TO LET GO!
"IT HEARD US... IT'S LOOKING FOR US!"
CAN WE FIGURE THIS OUT LATER? YOU KNOW, IF YOU DON'T GET US KILLED FIRST?
FOR A PAIR O' GENIUSES, YOU TWO ARE ACTING REAL STUPID!

OH, GREAT, WE'RE HERE.
WE'RE... NOT GONNA MAKE IT OUT OF THIS, ARE WE?

LEVEL FOUR

CREATE YOUR CHARACTER

NAME: MEL

FACE

BODY

HAIR

STRENGTH

VITALITY

CHARISMA

INTELLECT

AGILITY

LUCK

WHY ARE WE HIDING IF THEY CAN'T SEE US?
'CUZ NOT HIDING FEELS STUPID?
WE GOTTA GET IN THERE, THOUGH.
CAN'T WE WALK IN THE FRONT DOOR? WE'RE INVISIBLE.
NO. THEY MIGHT NOT BE ABLE TO SEE US, BUT THEY CAN FEEL US IF WE GET TOO CLOSE, TOO MANY OF THEM.
DON'T WORRY, I PLANNED FOR THIS. FOLLOW ME.

THAROOOM
DARHOOOM
KRAKRUUNK
SHE DUG A SECRET TUNNEL UNDER THE SCHOOL!?
WHAT DID I TEL--
I KNOW, I KNOW. DOOMSDAY-PREPPER-PERSON.

WHAT NOW, FEARLESS LEADER?
YOU KNOW WHERE THE CONTROL ROOM IS, RIGHT?
SHOW ME.
THEY'RE JUST WALKING AROUND IN THE OPEN NOW?
THEY PROBABLY DON'T THINK THEY NEED TO HIDE ANYTHING FROM A BUNCH OF IDIOT KIDS.
NO OFFENSE.
THAT'S STONE INDUSTRIES TECH. MUM'S COMPANY!
WE NEED TO FIND OUT WHAT THEY'RE DOING WITH IT!
THEY'RE HEADED TO THE AUDITORIUM.
WHAT'S IN THERE?
OH. MAN ALIVE! THAT SMELL AGAIN!
WHAAAAT THE HECK IS IT?!
ROTTEN EGGS. LIKE THE COMPUTER ROOM!

THE AUDITORIUM'S BEEN CLOSED SINCE THE ROBO-- **ANDROID** ATTACK. GUESS THIS IS WHY...
...I KNEW THEY WERE **BUILDING SOMETHING.**
UGH. DO I WANNA KNOW?
THIS DEVICE LOOKS LIKE A...GIANT 3D PRINTER.
AND THIS GOO IS...ORGANIC. **SOME SORT OF INCUBATOR?**

YUCK-YUCK- **YUUUUCK!**
DID YOU JUST TOUCH AN UNKNOWN CHEMICAL COMPOUND WITH YOUR **BARE HANDS?**
I WANTED TO SEE HOW GOOEY IT WAS.
VERY. IT'S VERY GOOEY.
ALRIGHT, FOCUS. **WE NEED TO GET TO THE CONTROL CENTER.**

THE WALL'S BRICKED UP. THERE WAS AN ENTRANCE THAT LED TO THE SUB-BASEMENT. THAT'S WHERE THE CONTROL ROOM IS.
STOP!
I KNOW WE'RE INVISIBLE, BUT IF WE SMASH THAT WALL, THEY'RE GONNA HEAR IT, RIGHT? THERE ARE GOONS ALL OVER!
OKAY, NEW PLAN...

TOBA, PUT ON THE BSP-PAK.
I'LL BREAK DOWN THE WALL. WHEN THE GOONS COME, THEY WON'T SEE YOU. MEL, ROMY, AND I WILL LEAD 'EM AWAY.
WHERE WILL YOU GO?
WE'LL GO TO THE ROOF, SEE IF WE CAN DESTROY THE TRANSMITTER DISH.
THAT WAY, EVEN IF SOME-THING...HAPPENS TO YOU IN THE ELSEVERSE--
WE STILL STOP THE SIGNAL. SAVE THE TOWN.
I GET IT. IT'S A GOOD PLAN
DARHOM!
'ELLO CHAPS! 'AVEN'T SEEN A SECRET UNDERGROUND BASE LYING AROUND ANYWHERE, 'AVE YA?
BORK!
BORK!

COME ON, KEEP UP, WE GOTTA LEAD THEM AWAY FROM TOBA!
ARE THEY TAKING THE BAIT?
UH. YEAH. I THINK THEY TOOK THE BAIT.
THEY TOOK ALL THE BAIT.
DON'T LET US DOWN, KID...

"...DON'T YOU DARE LET US DOWN."
I CAN'T LET THEM DOWN. FIND DAD, THEN SAVE THE TOWN.
HERE GOES NOTHING.
klik
I'M COMING, DAD. I'LL SAVE YOU.
klak
FRRRREEEITZZ

HEAVE!
HEAVE! HEA--
WE'RE HEAVING, YOU THINK WE DON'T WANT TO HEAVE?
PWHAMP
GOT THE DOOR!
THERE'S WAY TOO MANY OF 'EM.
NO WAY WE GET TO THE ROOF PAST THAT MOB!
I--I SAW MY MOM AND DAD OUT THERE!
ME TOO! OUR FOLKS WANT TO TEAR US APART JUST AS MUCH AS EVERY OTHER ZOMBIE OUT THERE.
WELL... WHAT DO WE DO?
KEERASHK
WE IMPROVISE.
YOU TWO AREN'T AFRAID O' HEIGHTS, RIGHT?

EWON! I'VE COME FOR MY FATHER!
I'M NOT AFRAID OF YOU!
WHERE IS EVERYONE? WHERE ARE EWON'S GUARDS?
TOBA!

IS THAT YOU?!
DADDY!
MY BEAUTIFUL BOY!
OMO MI! IT'S GOOD TO SEE YOU AGAIN!
YOU WERE ***BIGGER*** LAST TIME I SAW YOU. I EXPECT YOU'VE ***COME FOR THE SWORD?***
BIGGER? HOW COULD I HAVE BEEN BIGGER?
WHAT SWORD? I'VE COME FOR YOU. ***I CAME TO SAVE YOU.***
OH...OF COURSE. YOU DON'T KNOW. ***FOR YOU, IT HASN'T HAPPENED YET.***
WHAT YEAR IS IT?
2022...WHAT ARE YOU TALKING ABOUT, DAD?
WH-WHERE ARE WE GOING?
COME ON! THERE'S NO TIME TO WASTE!
WE MUST GO TO THE OBA'S PALACE. ***IT'S WHERE WE HID IT,*** AFTER ALL.

"WHERE WE HID WHAT?"
"WHERE WE HID THE EBEN SWORD. THE WEAPON WE FORGED TO DEFEAT EWON!"
BORK!
I KNOW, I KNOW. WE'RE ALMOST THERE. GOOD BOY.
MY MOM -PANT- WANTS ME TO BE A DOCTOR.
SHE...SHE DOESN'T KNOW I'M ON THE WRESTLING TEAM. -PANT-
YOU'D THINK MY ARMS WOULD BE -PANT- STRONGER, BUT -PANT- THEY FEEL LIKE GIANT WET NOODLES!
WHEN I'M AT HOME, I HIDE -PANT- MY TRACKSUIT FROM HER.
I BOUGHT -PANT- MEDICAL TEXTBOOKS JUST TO LEAVE LYING AROUND THE HOUSE FOR HER TO FIND.
DUDE... ARE YOU BARING YOUR SOUL?!

WE MIGHT DIE, IT FEELS LIKE THE RIGHT TIME FOR IT!
COULD YOU TWO SHUT UP?
BORK!
BUT YOU KNOW WHAT THE WORST THING ABOUT IT IS?
I GOT BORED, SO I -PANT- STARTED READING SOME OF THE MEDICAL BOOKS.
YOU KNOW. FOR FUN. AND I HAD FUN!
I DON'T WANNA GROW UP TO BE A DOCTOR!
I'D BE MORE WORRIED ABOUT GROWING UP THE NEXT TEN MINUTES...
...'CUZ THE ROOF...
...IT'S PRETTY HEAVILY GUARDED.
WHY DO YOU THINK I NEVER TRIED THIS BEFORE?

"FOCUS EVERYBODY, WE GOTTA GET TO THE TRANSMITTER, IN CASE TOBA FAILS."
IN A FUTURE THAT HASN'T HAPPENED YET, YOU AND MUM HELPED ME REBUILD THIS PLACE...ALL OF THIS!
DAD, I DON'T UNDERSTAND...
THE ELSEVERSE, TOBA!
A LIVING VIRTUAL CONSTRUCT THAT PRESERVES OUR CULTURE.
I BUILD THIS? HOW CAN YOU KNOW WHAT HAPPENS IN THE FUTURE?
TIME MEANS NOTHING IN THE ELSEVERSE. TELL ME, ARE YOU IN THE PRESENT, FUTURE, OR THE PAST RIGHT NOW?
MY...BODY'S IN THE FUTURE. MY MIND'S IN THE PAST--
--AND YET THE PRESENT, TOO!
HADN'T THOUGHT OF IT THAT WAY...
EXACTLY! WE'LL USE THE ELSEVERSE TO EXPLORE AND KEEP ALIVE OUR HISTORY, IN A WAY NO ONE EVER IMAGINED.
OF COURSE... WE ALSO ENCOUNTER DANGERS NO ONE EVER IMAGINED.
DANGERS... LIKE EWON?
YES, LIKE EWON. THAT'S WHY WE DESIGNED A WEAPON POWERED BY THE BONDS OF FELLOWSHIP; THE EBEN SWORD.
WE HID IT AWAY, LONG AGO, IN A CHAMBER IN THE UNDERCITY.

HOW DID YOU END UP IN THE ELSEVERSE?
EWON TRAPPED MY MIND WHEN I TOUCHED THE SPHERE YOUR MUM AND I FOUND. HE TRIED TO MAKE ME HELP HIM ESCAPE.
I REFUSED. YOU SEE, HE NEEDS A PHYSICAL BODY TO EXIST IN OUR WORLD, AND HE HAS NO WAY OF BUILDING ONE.
HE USED MY BODY TO TRICK MEREDITH STONE INTO BUILDING DEVICES THAT CONTROL THE PEOPLE OF BUCKHEAD. I DON'T KNOW WHY...
DAD, THE ADULTS ARE BUILDING SOME-THING WEIRD IN THE AUDITORIUM! IT LOOKED LIKE AN ORGANIC 3D PRINTER.
OF COURSE! IT'S HOW EWON INTENDS ***TO BECOME FLESH AGAIN IN THE REAL WORLD.***
GIVE ME YOUR STAFF, AND TAKE A STEP BACK!
THOOM THOOM THOOM
KERRRAK

GOTTA GET TO THE TRANSMITTER!
HNGG! THEY GOT ME! THEY GOT ME!
DAMN YOU, SPAGHETTI ARMS!
I...AGGCK! I CAN'T GET FREE!
TOO MANY OF THEM.
I GOTTA GET THROUGH!

THAT'S A *BOTTOMLESS PIT,* DAD.
AH! ONLY FOR THE MOMENT.
REMEMBER THE OLD YORUBA MYTH OF CREATION?
PINCH OF DIRT...
AND...I HAVE IT HERE SOMEWHERE ...*AH!*
THERE IT IS, A FRESHLY LAID EGG!
INTO THE VOID WITH YOU!
THERE'S EARTH DOWN THERE NOW.
YOU DESIGNED THE SOLUTION TO THAT QUEST...IN THE FUTURE.
ERM...ALRIGHT, I'LL HEAD DOWN. THEN WE CAN BOTH GET OUT OF HERE, RIGHT?
GO ON. THERE'S NO TIME TO WASTE.

DID YOU GET IT? **DID YOU GET THE EBEN SWORD?**
QUICKLY, LET ME SEE IT!
WAIT. YOU'RE ACTING SO WEIRD... ***WHY?***
I'M SO SORRY, TOBA.
I LIED. YOU SEE...
I CAN'T COME WITH YOU.
WHAT? ***NO!*** WHY NOT?
I NO LONGER HAVE A BODY, TOBA. ***IT'S LONG SINCE WASTED AWAY.***
NO! NO! YOU'RE COMING WITH ME!
I'LL ALWAYS BE HERE FOR YOU, IN THIS PLACE WE BUILT TOGETHER.
NEXT TIME I SEE YOU, YOU'LL BE A LITTLE BIGGER
I'LL SEE YOU AGAIN SOON. PROMISE.
BUT NOW YOU MUST GO. SAVE THE PLACE YOU'RE BUILDING NOW.

"SAVE YOUR FRIENDS..."
YOU WANT A FAIR FIGHT? HNGG!
I'LL TAKE YOU ALL ON!
NO...THEY'RE GONNA TATTOO-CHIP ME!
BZZZZATT
THEY'RE... FROZEN.
BORK!
SHADOW! YOU GOT THE TRANSMITTER'S POWER CABLE! GOOD BOY!
ZZZT
ZZT
YOU MAY NOT BE A RECALCITRANT GENIUS OR MOONLIGHT AS AN UNDERCOVER DOCTOR, BUT YOU'RE PRETTY HANDY AT BREAKING THINGS.
WHAT? I READ BOOKS. THAT'S MY SECRET SUPERPOWER.
RIGHT...WELL, C'MON'--LET'S GO GET THE KID!

HEY, KID!
DAD!
WHOA, RELAX!
YOU ALRIGHT? WHERE'S YOUR DAD? DID YOU FIND HIM?
WE'RE... ALL IN DANGER.
NAH, I SHUT DOWN THE TRANSMITTER... WELL, SHADOW HELPED A LITTLE.
BUCKHEAD'S SAFE!
NO! WE'RE NOT. NO ONE'S SAFE.

"EWON HAS ESCAPED THE ELSEVERSE...
RRRHEAAARGH
"THE FIGHT FOR BUCKHEAD'S JUST BEGUN..."

LEVEL FIVE

CREATE YOUR CHARACTER

NAME: ROMY

FACE

BODY

HAIR

STRENGTH

VITALITY

CHARISMA

INTELLECT

AGILITY

LUCK

KRI-KRLA
KRI-KRLA
KRI-KRLA
KRI-KRLA
KRI-KRLA
KRI-KRLA
SO MANY PLAYTHINGS...
WH-WHO'S THAT?!
OH DEAR...
N-NO--
NOAAUUFGHH!
HUSSSSSS
SO...MANY HERE TO BIND AND PINION.

SO MANY SERVANTS...
KRRA-KRASH
MY MINIONS, I HAVE OBSERVED THIS WORLD THROUGH HUMAN EYES THESE MANY WEEKS, AND LEARNED MUCH.
BEYOND THIS CITY LIES AN EVEN GREATER BOUNTY. UNTOLD MASSES.
THEY HAVE NO PROTECTORS, NO ÒRÌSHÀ TO STAND IN OUR WAY.
BURY THIS PLACE IN WRECKAGE AND RUBBLE.
I WANT NO TRACE LEFT OF OUR ORIGIN.
DHOOM
DHOOOM

"WE WILL MOVE OUT, INTO THE WORLD!
"WE WILL FINALLY TAKE OUR PLACE AS THE RULERS OF THIS REALM!"
DHOOM
DHOOOM

DHOOM
DHOOOOM
YO, WHAT THE HELL IS THAT?!
THE AJOGUN. THEY'VE INVADED OUR WORLD...
...AND EWON CAME WITH THEM!
DHOOM
WHAT?! WHAT DID YOU DO?
I DIDN'T DO ANYTHING.
LOOK, I'LL EXPLAIN LATER. RIGHT NOW WE HAVE TO GET TO THE AUDITORIUM.
HEY, WHERE'S YOUR DAD?
HUH? WHY?
HE...HE'S STAYING IN THE ELSEVERSE, ROMY.
HE CAN'T COME BACK TO THE REAL WORLD ANYMORE... BUT HE'LL ALWAYS BE THERE FOR ME.
DHOOM
OH. JEEZ, TOBA, I--
I'M OKAY, ROMY. REALLY. WE HAVE TO GET TO THE AUDITORIUM IF WE'RE GONNA SAVE BUCKHEAD.
THERE'S SOMETHING IMPORTANT WE HAVE TO GET.

DHOOM DHOOM
SOUNDS LIKE THEY'RE TRYING TO BRING THE WHOLE BUILDING DOWN.
THEY ARE. EWON WANTS TO BURY THE ENTRANCE TO THE ELSEVERSE... AND US ALONG WITH IT!
WHOA! HOLD ON. OUR PARENTS ARE STILL IN THE BUILDING. ALL THE ADULTS ARE!
YEAH, AND THEY'RE PRETTY OUT OF IT. I MEAN THEY DID JUST WAKE UP FROM THE WORLD'S LONGEST NAP.
ALRIGHT.
WELL, WHAT DO WE DO, DARSHA?
MEL, YOU AND ME ARE GONNA ROUND UP THE ADULTS AND LEAD THEM TO THE PARKING LOT. ROMY, YOU GO WITH TOBA TO THE AUDITORIUM.
THIS THING BETTER BE IMPORTANT, KID.
"OH, IT'S IMPORTANT."
THEY REALLY DID A NUMBER ON THIS PLACE.
-GASP- WHO...IS THAT...?
BEVILACQUA!
IS HE...?

NO, HE'S ALIVE.
I KNOW FIRST AID. DON'T TELL MEL, SHE'LL MAKE FUN OF ME.
TOBA, IT'S LIKE...IT'S LIKE...
I KNOW, ROMY. LIKE HE'S A PRISONER INSIDE HIMSELF.
THAT'S WHAT EWON DOES. **WHAT HE'LL DO TO EVERYONE.**
THAT'S WHY WE NEED **THIS.**
THE EBEN SWORD.

DHOOM
DAHOOM
C'MON, PICK UP THE PACE!
WHEN WAS THE LAST TIME YOU FOLKS *RAN ANYWHERE?!*
MEL, THAT'S THE LAST OF 'EM!
THE BOOMING...
IT'S STOPPED!
BUT WHY?
THE BUILDING'S COMING DOWN!
TAKE COVER!

BKRRRRRRUMMBLE
KAROOOOOM

YOU SEE, MY MINIONS? NO RESISTANCE THIS TIME.
ALRIGHT, YOU SCUMBAG. YOU'RE GONNA PAY FOR WHAT YOU DID TO MY TOWN!
AAAARRGHH!
INSOLENT CHILD.
POK
DARSHA!
TH...THAT ALL YOU GOT?

ARE YOU... ALRIGHT?
DO I... HNGH...! LOOK ALRIGHT?
YOUR ARM'S BROKEN...
I'M FINE. SEARCH THE RUBBLE, SEE IF YOU CAN FIND TOBA AND ROMY.
EWON JUST... IGNORED US. LIKE WE WEREN'T EVEN...
HOW ARE WE SUPPOSED TO BEAT THAT THING!?
KRAKRUMP
ANYONE HURT? -KAHF-
I, UH... KNOW FIRST AID, -KAHF- I CAN HELP.
YOU TWO FINALLY DECIDED TO SHOW UP, HUH?
IS THAT... BEVILACQUA?
EWON'S HEADED OUT OF TOWN. HE'S GOING TO DO THIS TO EVERYONE.
HE WANTS TO TURN THE WORLD INTO MINDLESS SLAVES!
OKAY. HUDDLE UP. HERE'S WHAT WE'RE GONNA DO.

FITTZZZ
"HE MAY WANT OUT OF BUCKHEAD, BUT HE WON'T GET FAR. HE'S TRAPPED IN HERE, AT LEAST FOR A WHILE.
THANKS FOR VISITING BUCKHEAD Come back soon!
"REMEMBER THE DAMPENER I BUILT THAT CLOAKS THE BUNKER FROM GOONS AND ADULTS?
"THE ONE THAT STOPPED THE MIND CONTROL SIGNAL FROM REACHING THE OUTSIDE WORLD?
HUMHUMHUM
"...IT'LL ALSO KEEP HIM TRAPPED INSIDE BUCKHEAD.
FRATTZZ
FITTZZ
"COURSE, HE'LL FIGURE OUT WHERE THE SIGNAL'S COMING FROM EVENTUALLY..."
MINIONS, I SENSE A FORCE ENCASING THIS TOWN.
"IF HE DESTROYS THE DAMPENER, HE'LL BE FREE."
FOLLOW ME TO ITS SOURCE, MINIONS.
WE HAVE TO GET TO THE BUNKER BEFORE HE DOES.
WELL, WE CAN USE THE BUS, BUT THERE'S NO DRIVER...
I...CAN DRIVE.

OHGOD OHGODOH GOD!
I THOUGHT YOU SAID YOU COULD DRIVE!
I CAN!
VVVVRROOOOOM
I MEAN I'M PRETTY GOOD AT DIGI-RACER IV.
THERE ARE NO SCHOOL BUSES IN DIGI-RACER IV!
Y...YOU SAW YOUR DAD?
I'M SORRY, TOBA. I THOUGHT I COULD...SAVE HIM--
IT'S OKAY MOM. I SPOKE TO HIM. TRY TO REST.
HOW ARE YOUR FOLKS, DARSHA?
CONFUSED. I CHECKED ON ROMY AND MEL'S PARENTS, THEY'RE OUT OF IT.
NEVER THOUGHT I'D END UP BEING THE ONE TAKING CARE OF THEM.

HE WANTS ME TO BE AN ENGINEER.
BUT I WANT TO BE A STUNT-WOMAN.
AND THAT'S OKAY.
THAT'S OKAY. RIGHT?

I THINK YOU'RE GONNA BE A KICK-ASS STUNTWOMAN.

...AND I'M LIKE... MOM, EXPECT SOMETHING FROM ME!
YOU KNOW, OTHER THAN A MAJOR CASE OF EXISTENTIAL ENNUI!
OR MAYBE IT'S WELTSCHMERZ...
SCREEEEECH
I DUNNO. IT'S SOMETHING GERMAN!
OHHHHMYGOD! LOOK IN THE REARVIEW!
YEAH, THEY'RE HOLDING HANDS. SAW IT. CUTE.
NO, NOT THAT...
KRI-KRLA
KRI-KRLA
WE'VE GOT COMPANY!
DARSHA, I KNOW YOU LIKE TO GIVE THE ORDERS, BUT I NEED YOU TO GET THE ADULTS TO THE FRONT OF THE BUS!
PLEASE, JUST TRUST ME.
ALRIGHT, KID.
HEY, GRANDMA MEL!
YOU WANNA STEP ON IT?
ROMY! COME HELP ME WITH THESE GROWN-UPS!

CRASHK
KRI-KRLA
I'M READY FOR THIS.
OH JEEZ, I HOPE I'M READY FOR THIS!
FTZZZZCHAAA
IT JUST... EXPLODED!
KRI-KRLA
KRI-KRLA
GUYS. MORE OF THEM. WAY, WAY MORE...

THERE'S THE BUNKER, WE'RE ALMOST THERE!
JUST BRAKE, MEL... BRAKEBRAKE BRAKE!
KLIP
KLANG
SNIP
SNAP
KRA-CHRUMPH
I'M... ALIVE?
DARSHA, THE BEAR TRAPS WERE A TERRIBLE IDEA!
YEAH, MAYBE THE BEAR TRAPS WERE A BIT MUCH.
KRUNK
THE BUNKER'S FORCE FIELD IS KEEPING THEM OUT!
THEY CAN'T GET IN AS LONG AS THE DAMPENER HOLDS OUT.
LET'S GET EVERYONE INSIDE!

I DON'T HEAR ANYTHING.
MAYBE THEY'RE GONE?
ARE THOSE HOLES IN THE STREET?
YEAH...
THEY'RE UP TO SOMETHING.
WHY WOULD THEY TUNNEL UNDERGROUND LIKE THAT?
THE DAMPNER'S SIGNAL'S WEAKER UNDERGROUND...
DARSHA, THEY'RE TUNNELING UNDER THE HOU--
BRAKOOOM
IMPUDENT CHILDREN! I WILL BIND YOU EASILY.

NOT IF I HAVE--
AAARGH!
TCHIANG
THE SWORD'S NOT HAVING ANY EFFECT!
I DON'T UNDERSTAND! DAD SAID WE WOULD NEED THIS TO BEAT HIM.
SKLANG
GLANG
OH YES! HOW I'VE MISSED THIS.
THE LONELINESS, IT FEEDS ME. SUSTAINS ME!
HE'S FEEDING ON LONELINESS?
TOBA'S NOT ALONE...
SO LET'S SHOW HIM...
...MIND IF I LEND A HAND?

SORRY I'M LATE, EVERYONE...
JOSUE!
IT'S WORKING, KEEP THE BEAM TRAINED ON HIM!
FWWZZZZ
NNNNOOOOOOOOOO
WE DID IT.
WE DID IT!

TOBA?!
TOBA ADEKUNLE?!
COMCAP
I'M MODDING!
THE ELSEVERSE AGAIN?
YOUR FRIENDS ARE HERE TO TAKE YOU TO SCHOOL!
BE DOWN IN A SEC!

WHAT'S UP, BIG MAN?
I'M HEADING OUT TO WORK, OKAY?
LOTS TO CLEAN UP AT STONE INDUSTRIES.
OH, AND GUESS WHO'S RECOVERED AND READY TO GO BACK TO SCHOOL?
IT'S ALL A LITTLE FOGGY STILL, BUT I KNOW YOU ALL SAVED THE TOWN.
I...I WISH I COULD HAVE HELPED MORE...
YOU BELIEVED IN ME WHEN I NEEDED IT.
GOOD TO HAVE YOU BACK, BUDDY!

WHAT'S OUR FIRST PERIOD?
SOCIAL STUDIES...
...WITH BEVILACQUA!
YOU KNOW, I HEARD THEY'RE UPGRADING THE COMPUTER LAB AGAIN...
BORK! BORK!
THE END

COVER GALLERY

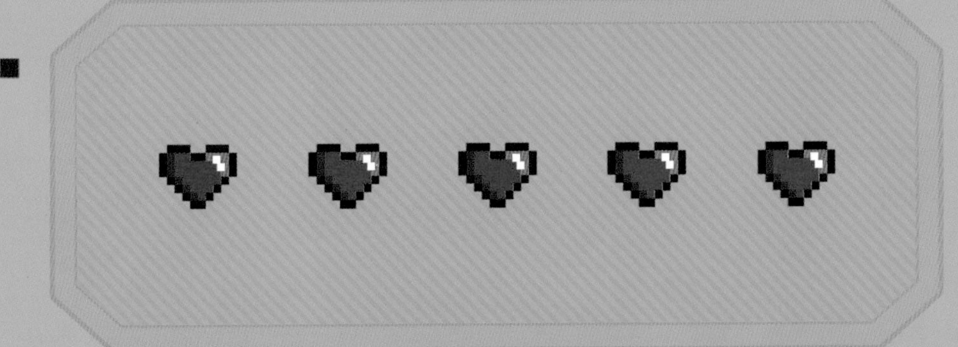

ISSUE #1 MAIN COVER BY **GEORGE KAMBADAIS**

ISSUE #1 VIDEO GAME HOMAGE COVER BY **SIMANGALISO SIBAYA**
WITH COLORS BY **NATALIA NESTERENKO**
& LOGO DESIGN BY **JILLIAN CRAB**

ISSUE #1 VARIANT COVER BY **KHOI PHAM**

ISSUE #1 FRANKIE'S COMICS
EXCLUSIVE VARIANT COVER BY **KIT BEUKES**

ISSUE #2 COVER BY **GEORGE KAMBADAIS**

ISSUE #2 VIDEO GAME HOMAGE COVER BY **SIMANGALISO SIBAYA**
WITH COLORS BY **NATALIA NESTERENKO**
& LOGO DESIGN BY **JILLIAN CRAB**

ISSUE #2 VARIANT COVER BY **SHOF COKER**

ISSUE #3 COVER BY **GEORGE KAMBADAIS**

BUCKHEAD 3

ISSUE #3 VIDEO GAME HOMAGE COVER BY **SIMANGALISO SIBAYA**
WITH COLORS BY **NATALIA NESTERENKO**
& LOGO DESIGN BY **JILLIAN CRAB**

ISSUE #3 VARIANT COVER BY **QISTINA KHALIDAH**

ISSUE #4 COVER BY **GEORGE KAMBADAIS**

ISSUE #4 VIDEO GAME HOMAGE COVER BY **SIMANGALISO SIBAYA**
WITH COLORS BY **NATALIA NESTERENKO**
& LOGO DESIGN BY **JILLIAN CRAB**

ISSUE #4 VARIANT COVER BY **YEJIN PARK**

ISSUE #5 COVER BY **GEORGE KAMBADAIS**

ISSUE #5 VIDEO GAME HOMAGE COVER BY **SIMANGALISO SIBAYA**
WITH COLORS BY **NATALIA NESTERENKO**
& LOGO DESIGN BY **JILLIAN CRAB**

ISSUE #5 VARIANT COVER BY MICHAEL OKORO

TOBA

JOSUE

DARSHA

MEL

ROMY

MEREDITH

BOLA

WOLE

MR. BEVILACQU

EWON

BLACK SUIT GOONS

AJOGUN

E HITS

BOOM! BOX

AVAILABLE AT YOUR LOCAL COMICS SHOP AND BOOKSTORE

To find a comics shop in your area, visit www.comicshoplocator.com

WWW.**BOOM-STUDIOS**.COM

All works © their respective creators. BOOM! Box and the BOOM! Box logo are trademarks of Boom Entertainment, Inc. All rights reserved.

Lumberjanes
ND Stevenson, Shannon Watters, Grace Ellis, Gus Allen, and Others
Volume 1: Beware the Kitten Holy
ISBN: 978-1-60886-687-8 | $14.99 US
Volume 2: Friendship to the Max
ISBN: 978-1-60886-737-0 | $14.99 US
Volume 3: A Terrible Plan
ISBN: 978-1-60886-803-2 | $14.99 US
Volume 4: Out of Time
ISBN: 978-1-60886-860-5 | $14.99 US
Volume 5: Band Together
ISBN: 978-1-60886-919-0 | $14.99 US

Giant Days
John Allison, Lissa Treiman, Max Sarin
Volume 1
ISBN: 978-1-60886-789-9 | $9.99 US
Volume 2
ISBN: 978-1-60886-804-9 | $14.99 US
Volume 3
ISBN: 978-1-60886-851-3 | $14.99 US

Jonesy
Sam Humphries, Caitlin Rose Boyle
Volume 1
ISBN: 978-1-60886-883-4 | $9.99 US
Volume 2
ISBN: 978-1-60886-999-2 | $14.99 US

Slam!
Pamela Ribon, Veronica Fish, Brittany Peer
Volume 1
ISBN: 978-1-68415-004-5 | $14.99 US

Goldie Vance
Hope Larson, Brittney Williams
Volume 1
ISBN: 978-1-60886-898-8 | $9.99 US
Volume 2
ISBN: 978-1-60886-974-9 | $14.99 US

The Backstagers
James Tynion IV, Rian Sygh
Volume 1
ISBN: 978-1-60886-993-0 | $14.99 US

Tyson Hesse's Diesel: Ignition
Tyson Hesse
ISBN: 978-1-60886-907-7 | $14.99 US

Coady & The Creepies
Liz Prince, Amanda Kirk, Hannah Fisher
ISBN: 978-1-68415-029-8 | $14.99 US